We're Very Good Friends,

My Grandma and I

P. K. Hallinan

For Gran, with love.

ISBN 0-8249-5379-7 (case)
ISBN 0-8249-5380-0 (paper)

Published by Ideals Children's Books
An imprint of Ideals Publications, a division of Guideposts
535 Metroplex Drive, Suite 250, Nashville, Tennessee 37211
www.idealspublications.com

Copyright © 1988 by Patrick K. Hallinan

Printed and bound in Mexico by RR Donnelley & Sons.

Library of Congress CIP data on file.

10 8 6 4 2 1 3 5 7 9

ideals children's books™
Nashville, Tennessee

We're very good friends,
My grandma and I.
We like to take walks . . .

And bake rhubarb pies.

And sometimes we'll just chat
For hours on end . . .

Or spend the whole day
Playing games of pretend.

We do lots of fun things,
My grandma and I.

We work crossword puzzles
And make up new words.

We paint funny pictures
Of colorful birds.

We even read comics
Then clip out the ads
And send off to Broadway
For all kinds of fads.

We get lots of great bargains,
My grandma and I.

But mostly we're happy
To spend the whole day
Just passing the time
In some wonderful ways . . .

Like seeing the seashore
And digging up sand,

Or watching a movie
Like *The Creature's Last Stand.*

Or maybe we'll drive
To a golf driving range
And laugh the whole way,
Singing "Home on the Range!"

We sing pretty well,
My grandma and I.

Then sometimes at night,
When the mood is just right,
We'll talk about places
And far distant lights.

And Grandma will sigh
How in days long ago
She had to say "no"
To a whole string of beaus.

We love to remember,
My grandma and I.

But then it's my bedtime,
So, quick up the stairs,
I run like a bunny
For a hug and a prayer.

And she always remembers
To kiss me goodnight
And to leave the door open . . .

And to light the night-light.

Yes, Grandma is special
In so many ways.

Her warmth just abounds
And surrounds all my days.

She's taught me to live . . .

And to stand very tall.

And I know she's the very best
Grandma of all!
So I guess you could say
Grandma's great love is why . . .

We're very good friends,
My grandma and I.